Gertrude is Gertrude is Gertrude **is**

Gertrude

Illustrated by **Calef Brown**

(who is calef brown)

**Atheneum
Books
for
Young
Readers**

**New York
London
Toronto
Sydney**

Gertrude is **Gertrude** is **Gertrude** is

Gertrude

Written by Jonah Winter

(who is jonah winter)

Atheneum Books for Young Readers

An imprint of Simon & Schuster Children's Publishing Division

1230 Avenue of the Americas, New York, New York 10020

Book design by Debra Sfetsios

The text for this book is set in Rockwell.

The illustrations for this book are rendered in acrylic.

Manufactured in China

First Edition

10 9 8 7 6 5 4 3 2 1

Library of Congress Cataloging-in-Publication Data

Winter, Jonah.

Gertrude is Gertrude is Gertrude is Gertrude/Jonah Winter ; illustrated by Calef Brown.—1st ed.

p. cm.

ISBN-13: 978-1-4169-4088-3

ISBN-10: 1-4169-4088-X

1. Stein, Gertrude, 1874–1946—Juvenile literature. 2. Authors, American—20th century—Biography—Juvenile literature.

3. Stein, Gertrude, 1874–1946—Friends and associates—Juvenile literature. I. Brown, Calef, ill. II. Title.

PS3537.T323Z97 2009

818'5209—dc22

[B] 2007001447

For the Bat Persons: Brooke, Karen, Fenner, and Maddy

—J. W.

For Mo and Kit

—C. B.

Gertrude

is

Gertrude

is

Gertrude

is

Gertrude.

And Alice

is Alice.

And Gertrude and Alice are

Gertrude and Alice.

Well it's like this.

You walk up the stairs, and there they are.

They are sitting in chairs

and there they are,

staring where they are **staring.** Not the chairs.

Chairs never stare.

Chairs are where you sit and stare.

Sometimes a bear **barely** sits in a chair.
But
but
but

wait a minute.

There's no bear there, heavens no.

There's just **Gertrude** staring and her chair.

And her chair is not even barely a chair,

no

no

no

no

no

it's a throne.

One
by
one
they
come
up
the
stairs

to greet her **majesty,**

Queen **Gertrude.**

Artists and artists and writers and artists.

Artists are artists and artists will be artists.

What will writers be we do not know.

Just writers probably.

Everybody talks.

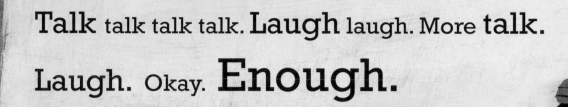

Talk talk talk talk. **Laugh** laugh. More **talk.**

Laugh. Okay. **Enough.**

And now it's time for tea.

Teatime is teatime.

And look who's here,

in time for tea.

It's **Pablo Picasso** the Spanish artist.

Pablo Picasso looks so angry but no.

Pablo Picasso is Pablo **Picasso.**

He just invented **Modern art**
which is not the same thing as **being angry**

but then again **maybe it is.**

Maybe it is
and **maybe it isn't.**
Then again **maybe it is.**
It's so hard to invent
Modern art.

Maybe it is
and
maybe it isn't.

Maybe.

But look
what a party.

Everyone who's everyone is at this party.
And everyone is everyone.
And if everyone is everyone, they must come to this party.

Oh look.

It's **Henri Matisse** with a beard beneath his teeth.
His teeth do all the smiling
but his beard does all the work.

That's his painting with the
bright bright very bright colors.
But he's such a quiet man.
He's such a bright quiet man, bright and quiet.

Oh no, here comes Basket.

Basket is a popular poodle.

Here, Basket. Sit.

Look, is that **Ernest Hemingway?**

Whisper whisper whisper.

It is, it is.

He writes novels on a typewriter. Sometimes he shaves.

Who are all these people and **why** are they here?

Well, where else would they be? **This is the place to be,** **yes** it is.

You see, this is **how** it works.

Gertrude does the talking and laughing.

And **Alice** makes sure that **Gertrude** is happy.

And while Alice sleeps, **Gertrude** is writing.

The night-time is the right time for writing,

so that's why **Gertrude** is writing and writing every night-time.

And in the morning, **Gertrude** sleeps.

And in the morning while **Gertrude** sleeps,
Alice is typing.

Alice is typing up Gertrude's writing,

whatever it is.

Oh, **Gertrude** writes whatever.

Pages
and pages
and pages
and pages
with words all over the pages.

My goodness, what fun.

What fun to write whatever words occur.

And now it's time to take a walk.

Hey, come back here, where are you going with that walk?

Well, I suppose we're taking this walk to the **art museum.**

And in the **art museum** we will talk of art.

And I suppose we will walk and we will talk some more, then sit in chairs.

That sounds nice, now doesn't it?

But suppose down the street from the museum there's an artist.

There's an artist making art, Modern art.

All art is modern when it's being made.

Gertrude likes Modern art because why not,

because, well, she's just

so modern.

Why not buy some Modern art?

Those crazy pictures **sure are crazy.**
Who cares?

A picture is a picture.
It can be **whatever** it wants to be.

It doesn't have to make sense.
It doesn't have to look like a waterfall,
not if it doesn't want to.

A picture can be **whatever.**

Why of course it can.

You can write **whatever you want to too**, if you're Gertrude.

A sentence can be whatever, if you're Gertrude.

You don't have to make sense (if you're Gertrude).

You can write **"rose** is a **rose** is a **rose** is a **rose"**

if you're Gertrude.

Why of course you can—if you're Gertrude.

You can write whatever you want to too, if you want to.

If you don't, fine. **Suit yourself. Don't blame me.**

And don't blame **Gertrude.**

Gertrude is having fun and you're invited. Don't be late.
And where is this party, if you please?

Well, it's **summertime,**

and the blossoms are blossoming,
and the garden is gardening, and it's time to be in the country.
Won't you please stop by in time for dinner please?

Okay time for you to leave.

Miss **Gertrude** simply must write tonight. Leave. Go. Out, out, out.

You see Miss **Gertrude** is a genius.

And a genius is a genius.

So what if no one understands a word she writes.

Some day they might.

But tonight Miss **Gertrude** is just

so so so happy as a baby, so happy.

And Alice is happy, happy as a mother, so so happy.

And the stars shine brightly outside the window.

That's a cow in a field.
It sleeps standing up.
It does not moo.

And here is another day of trees and sunshine.

Let's take a drive and **pack a picnic.**

Potatoes.

Mushrooms.

Strawberries.

Yes.

Thank you Alice for this food.

Thank you **Gertrude.**

Thank you for **driving.**
Thank you for driving a car named Auntie.

Thank you
for laughing.

Thank you

for writing.

Thank you for having fun when you write.

Thank you for this cow.

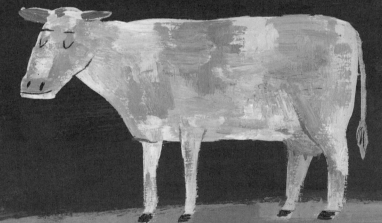

Who is Who is Who is Who

Gertrude's full name was Gertrude Stein, and she was a real person. She was a person, and she was a very, very, very famous writer. And her very famous writing was famous for being repetitive, playful, childlike, conversational, and often quite nonsensical. And her very famous writing has been imitated by many other writers, including the author of this book, whose title is an imitation of her most quoted line: "Rose is a rose is a rose is a rose." Gertrude Stein, the famous writer, is also famous for her companionship with Alice B. Toklas, one of the topics of her most famous book, *The Autobiography of Alice B. Toklas*, a book that also chronicles their influential friendships with the most important writers and artists of the era. Her other famous works include *Three Lives* and *Tender Buttons*. Stein was born on February 3, 1872, in Allegheny, Pennsylvania, of all places. In 1903 she moved to Paris, where she lived until her death on July 27, 1946. Often mocked in her lifetime, Stein is now praised for being among the most original and influential voices of the twentieth century.